The Snowbears of Lake Louise

David Chesky

Illustrations by Chris Bigelow

The Snowbears of Lake Louise by David Chesky
with illustrations by Chris Bigelow
"The Snowbears Anthem" music by David Chesky
lyrics by Rusty McGee and David Chesky
published by Chesky Kids, a division of Chesky Records, Inc.
P. O. Box 1268, Radio City Station, NY, NY 10101

Project Director Lisa J. Marks
Designed by Aldo Sampieri
Typography by Paul Kacchur

Printed and bound in Canada

ISBN 0-9658787-4-0

Summary: After falling into a ravine while skiing, an old couple wake up to find themselves in a land populated by magical bears whose job is to take care of the earth and keep the air, land and water clean for all creatures.

First Published in the United States by Chesky Records, Inc., New York, New York · Phone: 212·586·7537

I. Lake Louise

The old man sat at the desk in his room at the Chateau Louise, staring out at the mountains and the ice-covered lake. For the last forty years, he and his wife had come to Lake Louise every Christmas. First, only he and she came. Then, when they had children, they brought their children with them. Then their children had children, and the whole family would come up for Christmas vacation to be together, ski, and enjoy the beauty and tranquillity of Lake Louise.

Every morning, the old man woke up to the first rays of the sun and sat at the desk and wrote his stories before he and his wife went skiing.

As he wrote, he often gazed out the big window at the frozen lake. All around the chateau, the majestic mountains, blanketed by soft white snow, soared up into the sky.

This year was different for them because it was the first time in many years that they were alone for Christmas at Lake Louise. Their children had decided to take their families south for a warm winter's vacation. They had invited their parents, but the old man and woman kindly refused. They could not imagine a Christmas away from Lake Louise.

Today was no different from any other winter day at Lake Louise, except for the fact that it was the day before Christmas. The sky was cloudy, it was cold outside, and it was snowing. They watched the thick white flakes coming down outside their window while they ate a breakfast of tea and rolls. When the old man and woman got to the slopes, the snow was still falling gently, and it was very beautiful. The couple climbed aboard the ski lift and rode to the top.

All morning they skied. Then, at noon, they stopped for lunch. As they were enjoying their lunch, they talked about their children and their grandchildren and how they missed them. They always felt young again when they were skiing. So the old couple finished their lunch and went back out to ski. By now, the snow was falling harder and faster and the wind was picking up. Many of the skiers were leaving the slopes, but

the old man and his wife decided to make one last run down the mountain before they returned to Chateau Louise.

As they started down the trail, the snow was coming down so thickly that it was impossible to see the trail. They were desperately lost, and it was getting colder and darker on the mountain.

All of a sudden, they stumbled onto the steep side of the mountain. They lost control, and down they tumbled until they fell off the mountain into a ravine.

In this wilderness, the old man called out to his wife. He kept calling and calling until she heard him over the wind and started crawling through the thick snow to him. When she reached him, they grasped each other and cried until the tears froze on their faces.

By now it was pitch dark, and the old man and his wife feared that they were too far from the ski resort to be found by a search party. With the night came a bitter cold, and still the snow was piling up around them in the deep ravine.

The old man and his wife hugged each other to try to stay warm, but it was no use. The cold overcame them. Before long, they were lightheaded and fell into a deep sleep.

for the well-being of all the creatures who live on it and burrow into it and fly above it. For ages and ages, we did our jobs without any problems. But in the last hundred years, things have gotten very difficult for us. There was a time when we would freely go on the Earth's surface to be with the creatures, but that is much too dangerous now. Except for an occasional excursion, we live deep inside the Earth, where we control, manage, and try to balance as best we can what you call Nature. Perhaps you two can help us."

Then the old man and his wife had a long conversation with the two Snowbears Mawba and Penbra. They found them amazingly sophisticated and refined. They were perfect gentlemen—refined, witty, and intelligent. The old couple enjoyed hearing how the Earth really worked.

The Snowbears were in charge of the Earth, it seemed. They made all the managerial decisions, hiring the workers, directing the work, and constantly thinking about how to solve Earth's problems.

"For the next three days, Kanbra and Penbra will show you around, and let you see what we do," Mawba informed them. "After these three days, you will know what no other humans know—the truth about how the Earth runs and how unsure its future is.

With that said, Mawba wished them all a good night and left Penbra's Ice Castle.

IV. *Skybears*

he next morning, bright and early, Penbra and Kanbra woke the old man and his wife. Kanbra made them a delicious breakfast and served them Snowbear tea. The old man and his wife loved the taste of this sweet, hearty tea better than anything else they had eaten or drunk in the Land of the Ice Castles.

After breakfast, Kanbra gave each of them a special warm jacket because the place they were going to visit would be very, very cold—even colder than the mountain at Lake Louise. Then Penbra led everybody downstairs to the basement of the Ice Castle and into a large cave with many doors.

Penbra explained this was the Snowbears' secret Earth Cave. Every door in it led to a different part of the Earth. The Snowbears were the only ones who knew this secret form of travel, and they had guarded this secret since the beginning of time.

Penbra opened one of the doors and asked everyone to follow him. The door led into a small ice cave that was very cold. There was light coming from an opening at the other end, and they followed Penbra as he slowly walked toward the daylight. When they emerged through the cave opening, they found themselves on the top of a snow-covered mountain near the North Pole. It was very cold indeed. Even Penbra and Kanbra found it cold—and they were Snowbears!

Suddenly, as if from out of nowhere, a cute little blue bear that could not have been more than three feet tall came running over to them.

"How are you, Penbra?" said the little bear quickly.

Penbra said he was fine. He then turned to the old man and woman and said, "I would like you to meet Pip. He is a Skybear."

The old man thought, "What a funny little bear!" Pip was bright blue, and he moved and talked so fast it was hard to follow him. Penbra explained that all Skybears were like that. Living on this mountain near the North Pole, Skybears had to move and talk very fast in order to keep warm. He said that Pip, as the general manager of the Skybears, would show them around the top of the world.

Pip graciously conducted them to the other side of the mountain, where they saw what looked like hundreds and hundreds of white cotton sheets hanging on clotheslines. Hundreds of little blue bears were beating the sheets with brooms.

"How strange," thought the old man. But then Pip started to explain.

"We, the Skybears, are the keepers of the sky. We are responsible for taking care of and maintaining it. All the air in the world passes over this mountain. The dirt and dust get trapped on these sheets, and we shake it off the sheets with brooms. This is how the air becomes clean again.

"There was a time when we had to assign only a few Skybears to this duty and use only a few sheets. But now we need hundreds of Skybears and hundreds and hundreds of sheets to accomplish our work.

"There was a time when we had to work only a few hours a day, and then we could play in the snow. But there are not enough hours in the day to do our work anymore. Now we work so hard to keep the air clean that we are always tired."

The old man and his wife were stunned by this revelation. They felt very sorry for all the exhausted little Skybears.

Then Pip took them to a large cave where many Skybears were working at desks with computers.

"Well, this is interesting," said the old man. "What in the world are they doing?"

Pip explained, "This is the weather cave. These Skybears, who are sitting at the desks, regulate the temperature of the Earth. They have always done this. It used to be easy, but now it is getting very difficult. Since the beginning of time, we could

control the Earth's temperature without any problem, but about one hundred years ago things started to become unmanageable. Now there are so many strange chemicals in the air making the Earth hotter that we have to keep the smartest Skybears working on these problems night and day. But with all the cars, trucks, and factories, it is almost impossible to keep the Earth cool enough for healthy life."

He turned to Penbra. "Penbra, I am so tired and sad. We need more Skybears. We are too understaffed to keep things under control. Please speak to Mawba about this."

As they left the weather cave, Pip continued to instruct the old man and woman.

"Skybears have many jobs to do besides cleaning the air and regulating the temperature," he said. "Every day we have to make sure that the sky is the right color blue. It cannot be too light or too dark. If it gets off-color in the morning, we simply add or subtract the right amount of blue to restore it. Also, we Skybears are responsible for the changing seasons and deciding where and when it will rain and snow.

The old man remarked that this was a great deal of work.

"It seems like so much work," Pip agreed, "but since the beginning of time, we have managed it well. It's only in the last century that things have gotten out of hand."

Pip seemed so tired and overworked that the old couple felt sorry for him and the other cute little blue bears. But what could they do? They each gave Pip a warm hug in the cold, cold air at the top of the world, and sadly said good-bye.

Penbra then led them all back to the Earth Cave in the basement of the Great Ice Castle. They returned to Penbra and Kanbra's home where they had dinner together, and talked a bit about what the old couple had seen that day. Then they all went to sleep.

V. Waterbears

he next morning at dawn, Penbra and Kanbra came into the old couple's room to wake them. Once again, the humans and the Snowbears ate breakfast together and went down to the basement of the Ice Castle to enter the Earth Cave. This time Penbra opened a different door. Everyone followed him into another small cave, where light came from the opening at the other end. Penbra walked toward the opening and the others followed.

After passing through the opening, they found themselves on a beautiful tropical island beach. The ocean was a brilliant blue, and the waves made soothing sounds as they lapped against the sandy shore. The air was hot and humid and scented with the sweet perfume of colorful

tropical plants. In the middle of the island was a green mountain with cascading waterfalls. This place was so gorgeous that they decided to rest for a few moments to enjoy its beauty.

As they watched the ocean, the old man and his wife saw the strangest of strange sights. In the distance was a tall, thin, green bear riding a surfboard on one of the waves. He was actually an excellent surfer for a bear—or a human, for that matter. When the wave neared the shore, the bear jumped off and swam to the beach.

"Hey, what's happening!" he yelled. "Long time no see, Penbra and Kanbra. How have you been?"

"Fine, Goober," Penbra answered. "We've brought you two visitors. These are humans, and our guests."

Goober replied, "Wow, it's been a long time since I've seen one of them!"

"This is Goober," Penbra said to the old man and his wife. "He is the leader of the Waterbears."

"How strange this Waterbear is!" thought the old man. He was the exact opposite of Pip. Where the Skybear was nervous and excitable, this bear was cool, calm, and collected. In fact, he seemed to be too easygoing to be in charge of anything. But this was not the case at all. Goober was, in truth, a very hard-working Waterbear.

"Waterbears are all cool, calm, and collected by nature," Penbra explained. "Just as Skybears are hyper and quick-moving, and Snowbears are intellectual and elegant."

"Goober, can you show our guests exactly what Waterbears do?"

"Penbra, for you, anything," replied Goober.

The bear couple and the human couple followed the loping Goober through a rain forest and into a cave in the

mountainside. After they walked a few hundred feet, the space opened up into a gigantic cave full of water. Inside were hundreds and hundreds of Waterbears.

Goober explained, "We are the Waterbears. We are the keepers of all the oceans and seas of the world. It is our responsibility to take care of and maintain them. All of Earth's waters pass through this cave. Over here, in this cave, we clean the water before returning it to the oceans and the seas."

In the cave, hundreds of Waterbears were standing thigh-deep in the water, cleaning and sifting it with mining pans.

"First," instructed Goober, "we remove all the soil from the sea. Every year more and more soil gets washed into the sea and we must take it out. Then we use finer pans to screen all the pollution and chemicals that have been dumped into the sea.

"For thousands of years, we have done this without any problems. We used to have time to surf, play on the beach, swim, and build sandcastles. Did you know that the Waterbears taught the Hawaiian kings how to surf? A long, long time ago, when we could finish our work early in the day, it

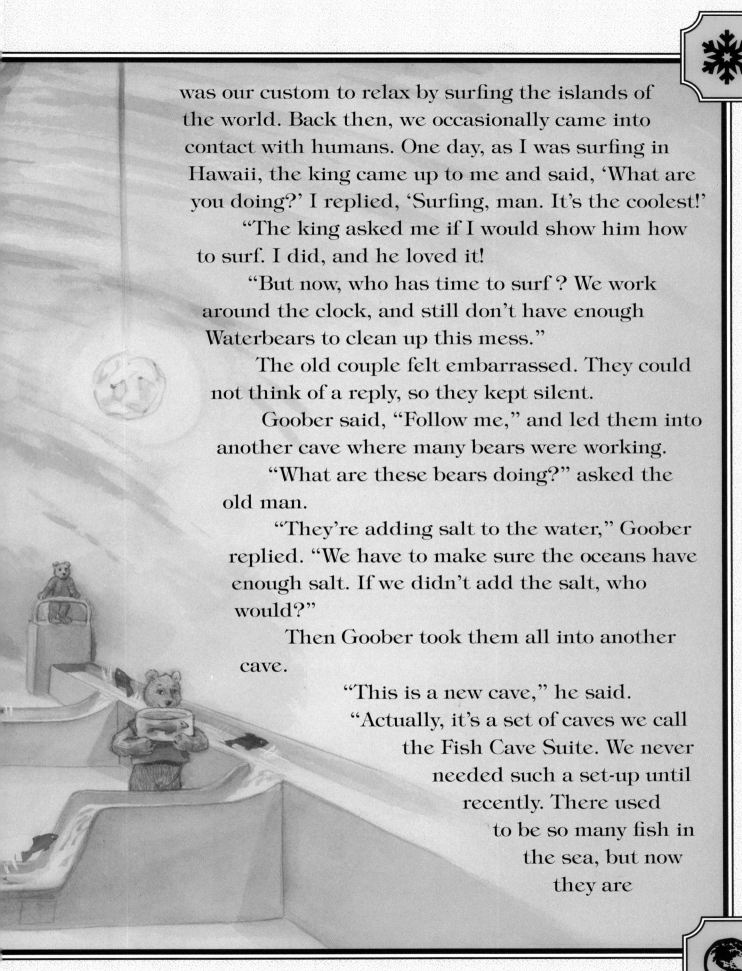

was our custom to relax by surfing the islands of the world. Back then, we occasionally came into contact with humans. One day, as I was surfing in Hawaii, the king came up to me and said, 'What are you doing?' I replied, 'Surfing, man. It's the coolest!'

"The king asked me if I would show him how to surf. I did, and he loved it!

"But now, who has time to surf? We work around the clock, and still don't have enough Waterbears to clean up this mess."

The old couple felt embarrassed. They could not think of a reply, so they kept silent.

Goober said, "Follow me," and led them into another cave where many bears were working.

"What are these bears doing?" asked the old man.

"They're adding salt to the water," Goober replied. "We have to make sure the oceans have enough salt. If we didn't add the salt, who would?"

Then Goober took them all into another cave.

"This is a new cave," he said. "Actually, it's a set of caves we call the Fish Cave Suite. We never needed such a set-up until recently. There used to be so many fish in the sea, but now they are

disappearing fast."

He waved a paw to the north. "This first cave is our fish-counting cave. All the fish in the oceans and rivers and lakes and streams pass through it, and we count them to see how many fish there are in the world. Every year there are fewer and fewer."

Goober turned and waved a paw to the south. "Now in this cave over here, the Waterbears are introducing young girl fish to young boy fish. We hope they will like each other and maybe even marry."

Then, grandly, he waved a paw to the west. "And finally, in this cave, the Waterbears are performing fish marriages. We are trying to marry as many fish as quickly as we can so we can increase the fish population." He sighed. "The problem is so many fish are tired and listless nowadays from breathing polluted water that they can't be bothered with starting a family.

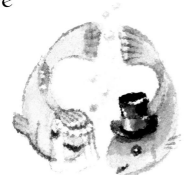

"All the Waterbears are tired and overworked too," said Goober. "We would like some time off so we could swim and do a little surfing again."

The old man and his wife told Goober they would try to do something when they returned home, but the reality was that they probably could not be of much help.

Penbra thanked Goober for his hospitality, and then he and Kanbra and the old man and his wife headed back to the Earth Cave and the Ice Castle.

It had been a long day and the old couple were very tired. So Kanbra made them a quick dinner and they went to bed early.

VI. *Earthbears*

On the third day, Penbra and Kanbra woke the old man and his wife early and brought them breakfast with the delicious Snowbear tea. For the third time, they descended to the Earth Cave in the basement of the Ice Castle. Penbra led them to a different door and opened it and they walked through. This time, there was no light shining in the distance, for they were in a dimly lit tunnel, not a cave.

"Where are we?" asked the old man, for he had been expecting another cave with daylight at the end of it.

"We are under the Earth, in one of the thousands and thousands of tunnels in the realm of the Earthbears," Penbra replied.

Just then, there was a loud rumble, and suddenly the largest bear the couple had ever seen was standing in front of them. This bear was not only huge, he was as brown as the dirt in the tunnel. On his gigantic head was a helmet with a flashlight on it. Except for its size, it looked just like the helmets coal miners wear.

Penbra said, "This is Flumby,

the leader of the Earthbears." Flumby greeted the old man and his wife in the deepest bear voice they had ever heard. It was so deep, in fact, it made them jump.

"We, the Earthbears, are the keepers of the land. All the forests and farms and meadows in the world have tunnels under them where we work. It is our responsibility to care for and maintain the land. I will show you around—but first we must get you some cub-sized helmets."

Flumby went off to consult with a couple of his fellow Earthbears, and they soon returned with the right-sized helmets for the old man and his wife and Kanbra and Penbra.

Then Flumby led them all into a large tunnel, where they saw many Earthbears at work. Flumby put his whistle in his mouth and gave three blasts. At the third blast, all the Earthbears started to sing. It turned out that Earthbears loved to sing as they worked and they worked very hard. First, they dipped their mops into buckets, and then they raised their mops together and started mopping the hairy ceilings of the tunnels. This they did again and again—dip and wash, dip and wash—all the while singing their work songs.

We are the Earthbears
And we dig and we shovel
And we shovel and we dig
And we dig, dig, dig all day
We clean the roots
And clean the dirt
There is no time to play
We clean the roots
And clean the dirt
There is no time to play
We are the Earthbears
Earthbears we are
We are the Earthbears
Earthbears we are

come back into the room and were smiling at them.

Mawba said, "It's a little gift from us."

The young couple said, "How can we ever thank you?"

Mawba said, "You don't have to. Now, it's time for you to go home."

So Mawba led the young couple back to the cave by which they had entered the Land of the Ice Castles with Penbra and Kanbra. There they kissed and hugged all three of the bears. Kanbra had tears in her eyes as she said good-bye to the couple she had once not wanted to know.

The young couple walked into the tunnel and out from the cave and into the mountains and snow of Lake Louise.

It was a beautiful day. The sun was shining and there wasn't a cloud in the bright blue sky as the young couple hiked up to the mountain ridge with ease.

With youthful energy, they climbed over the top of the mountain—and after that, no one knows what happened to them. But the legend goes . . .

There is a young woman who lives in a small house above Lake Louise. She is an environmentalist. She writes books, with the help of her young husband, about the whales and the seas and the rain forests. The couple travels all over the world to speak to people about saving the environment. They work hard. They also have many expenses, so when they are at home above Lake Louise, the husband works as a ski instructor to earn some extra money.

So, if you ever just happen to go skiing at Lake Louise,
and if you ever just happen to take a ride up one of the chair lifts,
and if ever you just happen to be sitting next to a ski instructor,
turn to him
and ask him about the Snowbears.

– The End –